The isla
g

Barbara Applin

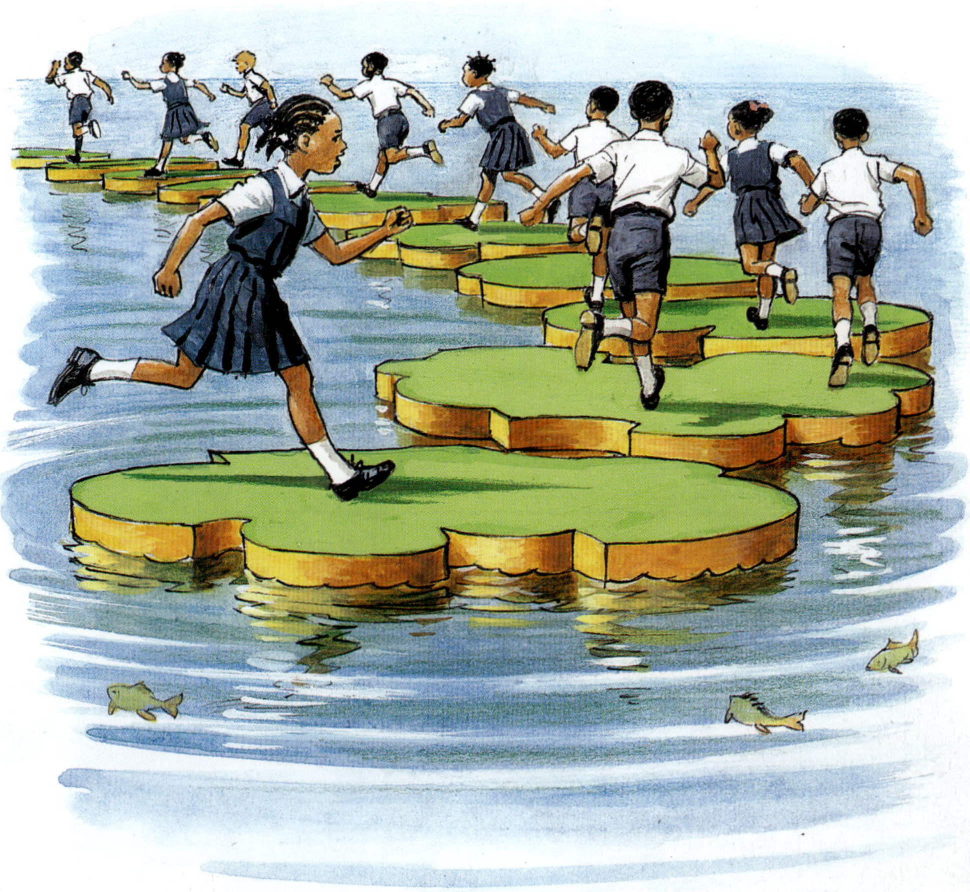

MACMILLAN
CARIBBEAN

Do you know this game?
It's silly but it's fun.
One child begins a sentence
and another child finishes it.
Remember the letter!

I went to Antigua ...

… and I brought back an alligator for my Auntie Alice.

I went to Barbados …

… and I brought back a balloon for my brother, Barnabas.

I went to Dominica …

… and I brought back a donkey for my Dad.

I went to Grenada …

… and I brought back a green grapefruit for my Granny.

… and I brought back a jazz band for my Uncle Jimmy.

I went to Montserrat …

AN

… and I brought back a mirror for my mother.

I went to Nevis …

… and I brought back a nutmeg tree for my nephew, Norris.

I went to St Lucia …

… and I brought back a seashell for my sister, Susan.

I went to Tobago …

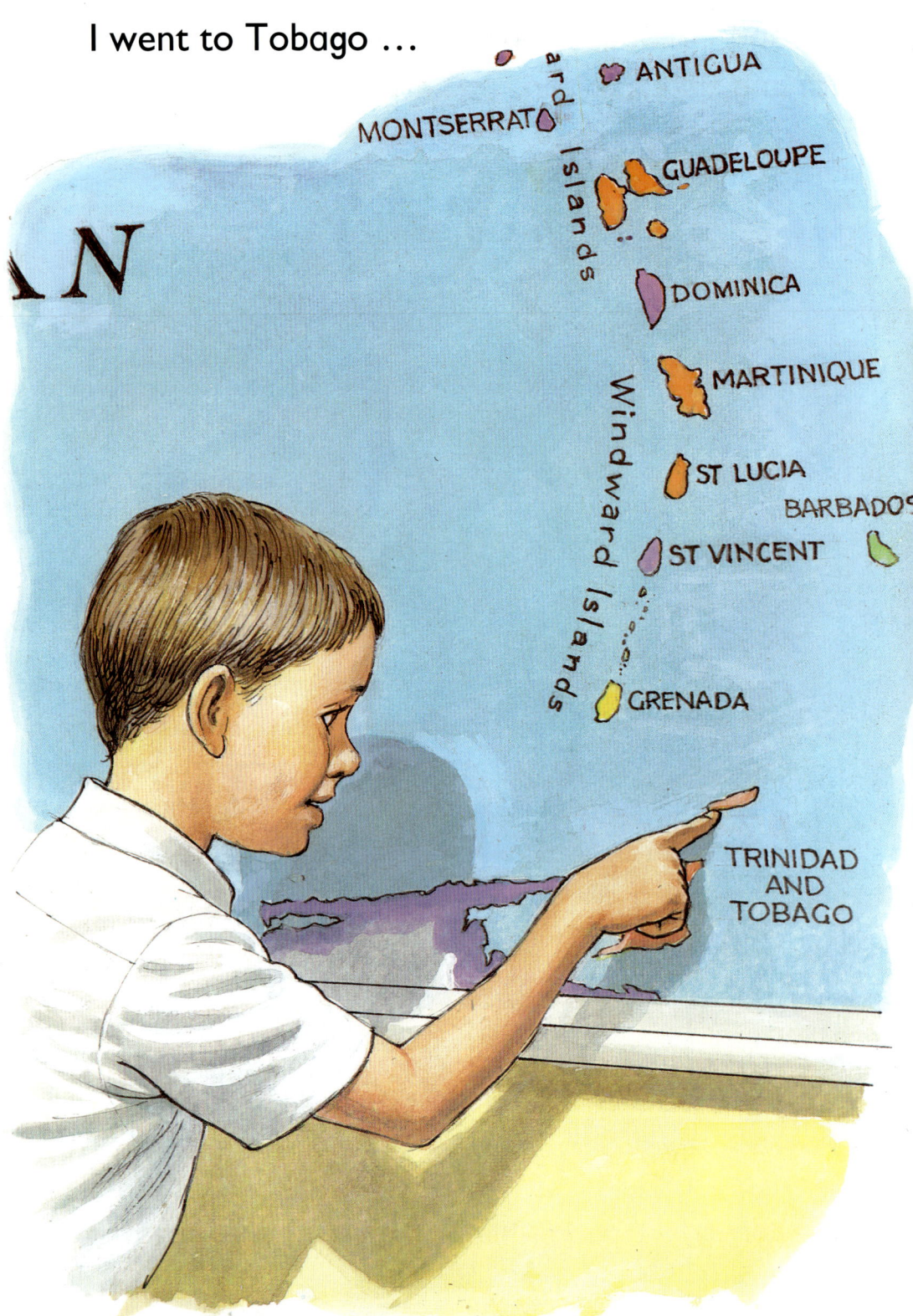

… and I brought back a turkey for my teacher, Miss Taylor.

I went to Trinidad …

… and I brought back a turkey for my teacher, Miss Taylor.

I went to Trinidad …

… and I brought back a tricycle for my dog, Trixie.

READY ... GO

I like fish   Marianna Brandt   0–333–71151–3
What's in Grandma's bag?   Marianna Brandt   0–333–71150–5
What can you see?   Marianna Brandt   0–333–71414–8
Say it! Do it!   Gail A Porter   0–333–73977–9
Malika's bath   Clare M G Kemp   0–333–73979–5
The toy that got away   Luke Warm   0–333–77451–5
Look about you   Gail A Porter   0–333–77113–3
The wart-hog trap   Clare M G Kemp   0–333–78993–8
Baby trouble   Clare M G Kemp   0–333–78994–6
Palms to clap   Janaki Sastry   0–333–78995–4
Memuna's baby   Adwoa A Badoe   0–333–79778–7
The little hairdresser   Nola Turkington   0–333–79827–9
Welcome, Lula!   Nola Turkington   0–333–79829–5
Mango tango   Clare M G Kemp   0–333–92086–4
What is sand?   Clare M G Kemp   0–333–92087–2
The twins   Barbara Applin   0–333–92088–0

Kiki and the storm   Shelley Davidow   0–333–69885–1
The river   Shelley Davidow   0–333–69884–3
A game with Granny   Rita Wooding   0–333–71413–X
Where is Zami?   Beverley Naidoo   0–333–72490–9
Happy Birthday, Joel!   Clare M G Kemp   0–333–73978–7
Can a car walk?   Kweku Duodu Asumang   0–333–78996–2
I can run fast   Gail A Porter   0–333–78997–0
The ice-cream river   Margaret House   0–333–78998–9
Monster in the bathroom   Clare M G Kemp   0–333–77114–1
Kuda's rainbow ball   Stephen Alumenda   0–333–79830–9
Kojo and the hen coop   Kweku Duodu Asumang   0–333–79831–7
Grandpa, who is Kakai?   Kwasi Koranteng   0–333–79777–9
Lindile and the red hen   Nola Turkington   0–333–79779–5
Go barefoot   Joanne Johnson   0–333–77603–8
Don't do that!   Barbara Applin   0–333–92090–2
The island-hopping game   Barbara Applin   0–333–92089–9

© Copyright text Barbara Applin 2001
© Copyright illustrations Macmillan Education Ltd 2001

All rights reserved. No reproduction, copy or transmission of this publication may be made without written permission.

No paragraph of this publication may be reproduced, copied or transmitted save with written permission or in accordance with the provisions of the Copyright, Designs and Patents Act 1988, or under the terms of any licence permitting limited copying issued by the Copyright Licensing Agency, 90 Tottenham Court Road, London W1P 9HE.

Any person who does any unauthorised act in relation to this publication may be liable to criminal prosecution and civil claims for damages.

First published 2001 by
MACMILLAN EDUCATION LTD
London and Oxford
Companies and representatives throughout the world

www.macmillan-caribbean.com

ISBN 978-0-333-92089-3

10 9 8 7 6 5 4 3 2
10 09 08

This book is printed on paper suitable for recycling and made from fully managed and sustained forest sources.

Printed in Malaysia

A catalogue record for this book is available from the British Library.

Illustrations by DONALD HARLEY/BL Kearley Ltd